Leigh Hodgkinson

BOOK HOSPITAL

SIMON & SCHUSTER

London New York Sydney Toronto New Delhi

Hi there – I'm a book!
Sure, I know I look a bit tatty but that's OK.
In fact, I actually LIKE being a bit tatty
as it means I am loved and read **a lot**.

Yes, most of the time it is
pretty great being a book.

THE BOOK NEXT DOOR

THE BALLET DANCING ASTRONAUT

THE BURP TREE

THE JELLY TRACTOR

THE SECRET NOTHING

THE INVISIBLE COLOUR

THE ICE-CREAM MAGNET

You get to tell all sorts of AMAZING stories.

BOOK HOSPITAL

SLOTH SCHOOL

THE CAT BICYCLE

THE FUTURISTIC DINOSAUR

THE CHIP GHOST

THE BAD WITCH

THE SHY NIT

HAIRY SCARY MONSTER

SPOTTY LIGHTHOUSE

THE MONKEY MYSTERY

THE BORING BOOK

THE BEIGE SUBMARINE

THE BOUNCY SLUG

THE JAZZ ROBOT

PENCIL DOG

PIRATE PYJAMAS

THE SINGING ANT

PINEAPPLE BRAIN

THE SILLY PENGUIN

THE TEENY WEENY ADVENTURE

There are books with stories about bad witches . . .

THE BAD WITCH

The Bad Witch had great fun turning pretty flowers into warty old frogs.

. . . who turn out to be **good** in the end.

She didn't know how to turn them back again.

I'm sorry.

That made her feel bad.

But it didn't matter anyway, as the pretty flowers preferred being warty old frogs.

Or there are books with stories about
HAIRY SCARY monsters . . .

. . . who turn out to be not so scary
(but still hairy) in the end.

Or there are books with stories about
teeny weeny adventures . . .

THE TEENY WEENY
ADVENTURE

. . . which turn out to be BIG,
GIGANTIC adventures in the end.

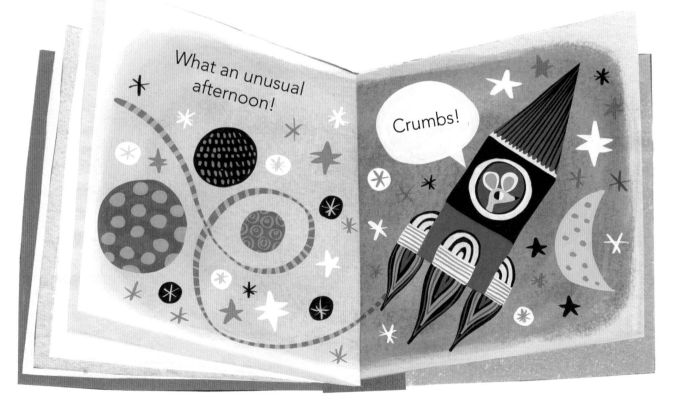

But if you ask me, the BEST bit about being a book . . .

. . . is just to hang out
with your friends.

I wish it could be like this all of the time
but, unfortunately for some books . . .

it isn't.

Sometimes a good book just
happens to be in the wrong place
at the wrong time.

Like this one book I heard about
who got scribbled on.

Not every book is a colouring book
you know, kids.

Or this really nice book I know, who got covered
in strawberry yogurt and went all sticky
and stuck together.

Poor little guy – a book should never be
all sticky and stuck together.

And there was this other book from the library across the road who got nibbled by little teeth . . .

Yes, actual real-life teeth . . . can you believe it?

Wow, I'm so lucky that nothing like that
has ever happened to me.

Uh-oh . . .
looks like I spoke
too soon . . .

HELP!

Ouch. Too late.

My LAST and MOST IMPORTANT page
has been ripped out.

GONE!

BOOK HOSPITAL

Oh no . . . This is a COMPLETE book emergency!

And when there's a COMPLETE book emergency,
there's only one place to go . . .

BOOK
HOSPITAL,
here
I
come!

At Book Hospital there are lots of
nice doctors and nurses all ready and waiting to help.

No need to worry – it will all be OK!

Everyone soon starts to
feel much better

and will get to go home
where they belong.

Everyone except me that is.

BOOK HOS

Oh dear, it looks like the end
of my story is lost forever.

Well, would you look at
that – visitors!

And also,
my LAST and most
IMPORTANT page . . .
Thank you!

After some very careful sticky tape action, I'm ready to go back home again.

Just in time for the BEST part of the day . . .

. . . bedtime! Yippee!

So that's it.

That's my story –
my COMPLETE story.

THE BOOK NEXT DOOR
THE BALLET DANCING ASTRONAUT
THE BURP TREE
THE JELLY TRACTOR
THE SECRET NOTHING
THE INVISIBLE COLOUR
THE ICE CREAM MAGNET
THE JOKE DICTIONARY
THE BRUSSELS SPROUT MACHINE
THE CAT BICYCLE
SLOTH SCHOOL
THE FUTURISTIC DINOSAUR
THE CHIP GHOST
THE BAD WITCH
THE SHY NIT
HAIRY SCARY MONSTER
SPOTTY LIGHTHOUSE
THE MONKEY MYSTERY
THE BORING BOOK
THE BEIGE SUBMARINE
THE BOUNCY SLUG
THE JAZZ ROBOT
PENCIL DOG
PIRATE PYJAMAS
THE SINGING ANT
PINEAPPLE BRAIN
THE SILLY PENGUIN
THE TEENY WEENY ADVENTURE
THE SPOON TREE

BORED BANANA
THE SQUARE EGG
SNAIL PRINCESS
THE BIG SNEEZE
THE EGG

THE BURP TREE
THE INVISIBLE TRUMPET
THE VERY SERIOUS JOKE BOOK

Oh, just one more thing.
Yes, I know, you're probably not
one of those . . .

. . . young scribblers,
yogurt dippers,

keen nibblers
or page rippers, are you?

And I'm guessing **you** probably know this
anyway, but please look at my LAST
and MOST IMPORTANT page . . .

your books.

to your books.

your books.

And if you do, your books will take you on magical journeys that you'll never forget.

Also by Leigh Hodgkinson: Pencil DOG

SIMON & SCHUSTER
First published in Great Britain in 2021 by Simon & Schuster UK Ltd
1st Floor, 222 Gray's Inn Road, London WC1X 8HB
Text and illustrations copyright © 2021 Leigh Hodgkinson

ISBN: 978-1-4711-6942-7 (HB) • ISBN: 978-1-4711-6943-4 (PB) • ISBN: 978-1-4711-6944-1 (eBook)
Printed in China • 10 9 8 7 6 5 4 3 2 1